Nutcracker Rich

June Seas

CAROLINGIAN
PRESS

Contents

For our Prince Richard

The Party

CHRISTMAS EVE AT LAST! The house smelled so delicious. The great table was moved aside so there would be room for dancing. Then many careful hands spread Mama's best linens, shining dishes and sparkling glassware. These were laden with holiday foods and sweets. There would be sinfully fragrant coffee and tea, and cocoa for the children. The children were already dreaming of the desserts they waited for all year.

Meanwhile Clara and Fritz were being dressed in itchy finery. Fritz complained about his velvet suit and tight shirt collar. Mama slicked Fritz's hair, but one little tuft of hair insisted on standing up stubbornly. Clara's hair was curled and tied into a ribbon. She loved her shining dress with all the ruffles and pleats and lacy collar! But she didn't care for the stretchy tights which never quite seemed long enough, and her shiny patent leather shoes felt like they pinched a bit all of a sudden.

Christmas Eve would be a long, late night. But they were so excited that neither had been able to rest during the scheduled nap time.

They were excited in anticipation of all the family guests who would arrive, relatives they rarely saw, cousins all dressed up like mini grownups; together they would gorge on sweets made over many weeks only for this night.

There would be gifts exchanged, toys and novelties. Aunts would kiss them and funny uncles do magic tricks. The children would listen to their elders' jokes and old stories.

By the time they headed out into the early night for church, they were very wound up. They settled a bit with the caroling and candles. As the family headed home it was snowing lightly, just enough to kiss them with a cold thrill of Christmas joy.

Clara followed Fritz, running into the great hall and sliding across the polished floor. They stood looking at the table in awe. They were hungry and the footed dishes stood one on another, piled high with the most beautiful food.

"Stop that!" Mama clapped her hands, and Papa told them to settle down. But the doorbell rang and their family started arriving, grandparents and people they knew as aunts and uncles and godparents, whether they were related or not, and children, boys and girls of all different ages and sizes, and little ones already crying.

There was so much noise, talking and laughing and drinking, and children running back and forth, or some hiding behind their parents. Clara drew them out with a smile and a kind hand, and Fritz was engaged in games already, hide and seek under the table and behind the coats. There was passing of plates, and a general rumpus. When guests gave their gifts, the children settled down on the floor to examine their new treasures. Fritz had a set of toy soldiers and was at war with his fellows. Soon the children were up and running around again with their treasures, riding the hobby horses, walking their dollies and pets.

So just in time came the dancing! Couples, big people and little people together, and the children in their own dances, partners and line dances. Colors swirled around the room, dresses twirled, everyone stood so straight and tried so hard together, they were like a magical kaleidoscope of human parts.

Now the children were feeling hot and flushed, a little sticky and chafed. They had eaten a few too many sweets and it was after bedtime already. Some disputes broke out between the children over the sharing of toys; some teasing, which was ordinarily borne with good humor, caused tears.

The clock suddenly struck the hour with an echoing gong, and the doorbell chimed. "Who could that be?" Mama winked at Papa, who opened to the door to one late guest.

Presents

A TALL, DARK SHADOW of a man stepped in from the snow, his long dark cape sweeping the cold air in. The crowd fell back, gasping. Mama took his hat and cape. He appeared frightening; with a patch over an eye, bristly gray frowning brows and mustache, a walking stick bearing a beady eyed winged creature atop it, he looked to be a villain.

"Mr. Drosselmeier!" Clara and Fritz ran to him and he leaned over and pulled a coin for each of them from behind their own ears. Drosselmeier was Clara's godfather and even though he looked scary to most children, he always manifested strange wonders when he appeared and disappeared at the oddest times. Drosselmeier tinkered with all kinds of clockworks, and invented the most wonderful machines. No one had seen his workshop, but he could produce marvelous toys, seemingly from nothing.

Everyone settled down in a large circle to leave plenty of room between themselves and Drosselmeier. He waved his stick in elaborate symbols in the air, and two giant boxes were pushed into the room. He tapped each with his stick and scurried away. The boxes opened like doors, and a pair of life-size puppet figures nodded and waved. When he pushed away the boxes, he wound up a giant key on the back of the dolls, and they could move on their own!

The audience cheered. The automatons shared a funny robotic dance, then flopped over and were lifted aside to make room.

Mr. Drosselmeier then presented Clara with a special doll of her own. The doll was a large wooden soldier prince, with a colorful dress uniform and hat, a strong square jaw, large eyes and shiny hair. His jaw was so strong, in fact, that he was a nutcracker. Drosselmeier produced nuts in the shell from his pocket and showed them how it worked, and everyone laughed and applauded. They shared the nuts smashed open by the prince, and then Clara held the prince in her arms in a big hug.

Fritz was feeling jealous and irritable. When the crowd resumed their socializing and enfolded Drosselmeier among themselves, Fritz galloped up behind Clara on his stick horse and grabbed the nutcracker prince out of her arms, riding off with it. She jumped up, chasing him with some of the other girls. Fritz galloped about and tossed the nutcracker to some of the other boys, who used him like a football, to keep him from the girls. It happened, by accident or on purpose, that the prince was dashed to the ground, and Fritz rode right over him, stomping on him, then ran away.

Clara cried out and scooped up into her arms the nutcracker with a broken jaw. Papa scooped up Fritz and took him off for a harsh scolding. Drosselmeier appeared at Clara's side and gently took the nutcracker to fix him. Clara ran off in tears.

But she returned, with a little dolly princess bed from her playroom, and knelt beside Drosselmeier. He returned the nutcracker to her. She cuddled him and tucked him gently into the little bed. Clara was feeling very sleepy too. Drosselmeier kissed the top of her head and swirled away into his cape, disappearing from the room.

Little ones had been dropping into slumber near the Christmas tree. A commotion began near the door, with the hosts delivering cloaks to guests, who began scooping up their sleeping little ones and heading out the door with smiles, hugs and thanks.

The room was empty now but for the twinkling tree and their own family. Papa carried the drowsy Fritz off to bed, and Mama brought Clara away to bed as well. Clara waved goodnight to her prince, slumbering in his little bed under the tree.

Shrinking and Growing

D URING THE NIGHT, THE windowed
doors blew open and a swirl of
snow blew into the room and over the
tree. Something, perhaps the blast of
cold, had wakened Clara, and she padded
down to the great room in her nightgown
and bare feet, shivering. She put another
little blanket over her prince, and pulled
a shawl from a chair, wrapping herself in
it.

Suddenly the clock bonged. As Clara sat with her little prince under the tree, the tree started growing! The ceiling of the room seemed to get farther and farther away until it looked like the night sky, it was so dark. And the sparkling Christmas tree grew taller, and taller and taller until Clara could hardly see the top! She looked up into its branches and saw the shining ornaments huge overhead like jeweled planets, and twinkling lights like the stars.

But here was her little doll bed, and her wooden prince, grown to lifesize! She climbed onto it and sat upon the white satin bedding, holding onto the brass bed footboard and looking around the room.

Do you think the tree grew? or did Clara shrink to the size of a little doll?

Clara heard scurrying, and a mouse, then another and another scampered into the room. But these were no tiny mice. No, they were giant mice, bigger than Clara! She shrunk under the covers but the mice with their sharp teeth and glowing eyes came threateningly close to paw at her.

At once, the prince next to her leapt from the bed and brandished his sword. He was flesh and blood, a handsome human soldier prince! He drove off the mice, but more and more flooded in, so many mice, and behind them, directing his army, was the great Mouse King. The Mouse King had five heads, a golden crown on each, and five glaring pairs of red eyes and five mouths of sharp snapping teeth.

The Prince was bravely whacking at mice with his sword, but there were so many. He ran about the room and rounded up Fritz's toy soldiers, who were now, of course, Clara's size. They marched courageously into battle behind the Prince. They fired their cannon which threw a ball into the midst of the mice, knocking many off their feet, and many scurried away.

Then the Prince fought his way to the Mouse King and was close in battle. The mouths in all the heads snapped and bit, and the nutcracker prince gnashed his teeth. But suddenly he was surrounded by mouse reinforcements!

Clara bravely followed her prince into the battle, and swung a stick horse through the mice, whacking them right and left. The Mouse King turned to her and snapped his teeth as she shuddered. The Prince pushed her out of his reach and she slipped and hit her head, falling unconscious.

When she awoke, she was upon her princess bed. The mice were gone. The Prince walked through the ranks, tending to Fritz's toy soldiers. When he saw her sitting up, he approached her and bowed.

"Your Royal Highness," he spoke. "Prince Richard, your obedient servant and defender to the death." He held out his sword to her, the two ends resting on his two hands. He then sheathed his sword, and held onto the footboard of the bed as a gust of wind blew at them.

A swirl of snowflakes blew into the room, and performed a beautiful dance swirling around for Clara. And now Clara saw that the sky was overhead, and she could no longer see the walls of the great room, but rather a fairy tale forest of Christmas trees.

Were those angels floating behind the snowflakes, singing the music of heaven?

The Land of Sweets

I MAGINE HOW STARTLED CLARA was to see suddenly appear, in the middle of this snowy forest, a sparkling, twinkling, pastel Sugar Plum Fairy! The Fairy teetered on top of an elaborate white throne, which looked just like the fancy royal icing on a tiered wedding cake. She fluttered her transparent wings and floated down, pointing with her starry wand to two royal filigreed chairs. The

Sugar Plum Fairy Queen smiled sweetly and spoke to Clara, but Clara could not understand the fairy; all she could hear was a gentle tinkling of bells.

Prince Richard bowed low to the Fairy and to Clara, and then handed Clara up the first step to her throne. The Prince tried to explain to the Fairy about their exploits against the Mouse King, and how they had arrived here, but she just shook her head, tinkling. So he mimed for her, acting out the battles with the mice.

The Sugar Plum Fairy Queen clapped her hands in delight, and bade Richard kneel before her. With her star she knighted the Nutcracker Prince upon his shoulders, kissed his cheeks, and pointed to his seat next to Clara. Clara's and Richard's hands just barely touched, on the edge, as they rested their arms on their thrones. They looked at each other shyly.

With a lovely curtsy flourish, the Fairy honored her two guests, and pointed her wand at the assortment of sweets piled in a circle surrounding them.

Peppermints, chocolates, marzipan, Danish treats, French patisserie, gingerbread, even tins and baskets of teas and coffees, spread across the horizon. All the gorgeous candies and pastries were decorated with delicate flowers hovering over the display.

As the Sugar Plum Fairy waved her little wand, one after another, the little delicacies wiggled and bounced and came to life! The beautiful figures depicted on the tins of Asian teas stepped out of their green countries and danced delicately for the Nutcracker Prince and Princess. Coffee from the tropics spilled out a sultry dance before them.

Wide awake, Richard and Clara eagerly watched each novelty perform its characteristic delights. There were acrobatic candy canes and elaborately decorated cookie people from many lands, just like the holiday cookie collections Clara's family and friends shared and traded. With each dance, the lovely desserts had presented Clara with a sweet for her, which piled in her lap. Clara began sorting these into her handkerchief to take home for poor Fritz.

Finally an enormous Mother Ginger cake tin climbed up on spindly legs and strode to the stage. She powdered her face and confectioners' sugar went everywhere! When she lifted her skirts, all the little gingerbread boys and girls scurried out and danced around her giggling and teasing. Richard and Clara laughed at all the family clowning, and tasted the sugar snowflakes made by Mother Ginger's frantic powdering.

By the time Mother Ginger had gathered up the gingerbread children and gone back to sleep in the corner, and the flowers had elegantly nodded in time to sweet waltzing music, Clara was feeling sleepy and missing her home. Richard, alert, asked Clara to join him in a dance, and as he held her and they twirled together, she fell into step with him as if in a dream, and everything around them seemed to disappear.

They were no longer tiny beings in an outsized world for giants. The toy wooden doll Nutcracker had earned his manhood, and Clara stood tall as a princess. When the stirring music of the dance ended, Nutcracker Prince Richard presented his gift to Clara: he held out his hands on which sparkled five tiny gold rings for Clara's fingers.

"But these—these were the crowns of the Mouse King!"

Clara awoke in confusion, in the chair by her own Christmas tree at home. Her little bed was empty. Toy soldiers lay scattered about. A fairy ornament near the top of the tree smiled down, and tinkled in a breeze from the open window. Clara ran to the window and looked out. The icy snowflakes kissed her nose. She looked away down the street, where a handsome young soldier walked. Clara waved wildly, with a sob catching in her throat. She could see his wide white grin as he waved back at her. He blew her a kiss, "'til tomorrow!" Then he turned the corner, walking away backwards so he could look back at her.

It was still dark. The clock chimed just the hour of one. Clara carefully closed the window, and saw the glint of gold on her fingers.

***

The End

Afterword

In setting down these words, I wanted to share the Nutcracker story with my godson. Many dance fans suggest that for children seeing the ballet for the first time, they value sharing a book or oral retelling of the story.

And what a story! An original Nutcracker and Mouse King tale is from E.T.A. Hoffmann; the original German and early translations are in the public domain, as are a subsequent adaptation by Alexandre Dumas, (French), and early translation. Tchaikovsky composed the music for a ballet inspired by the story, for the Czar and Russian audiences. The original and various choreographies of the ballet tell, through dance and set, their own versions modifying the tale.

I chose to share a brief original retelling in a little book suitable for sharing before the ballet, or on its own merit as a sweet holiday story. This is the classic tale, reimagined. And as always the characters—or was it Drosselmeier, or the Sugar Plum Fairy?— wrested the story from me and created their own performance.

Also By

Find more stories told in brief chapters
from Carolingian Press Books, including:
*Legendary Fairy Tales Reimagined, a
Chapter Book*, June Seas
*The Look of Things: Mystery of the
Haunted Library*, June Seas
True Tales of Ghosts, a Salt 'n' Pepper
Book , C.L. Vadimsky and S.L. Vadimsky

About the Author

June Seas has lived many adventures, including as a teacher, a children's librarian, and with her children and godson. She has seen many years of diverse performances of the Nutcracker ballet, and she reads and researches a lot. June works on her stories outdoors. Her life is just a beautiful dream.

Made in United States
Orlando, FL
26 November 2024

54515216R00024